PETUNIA'S

CHRISTMAS

Written and Illustrated by

Roger Duvoisin

Alfred A. Knopf · New York

THIS IS A BORZOI BOOK PUBLISHED BY ALFRED A. KNOPF

Copyright © 1952 by Alfred A. Knopf

Copyright renewed 1980 by Roger Duvoisin

All rights reserved under International and Pan-American Copyright Conventions. Published in the United States

by Alfred A. Knopf, an imprint of Random House Children's Books, a division of Random House, Inc., New York,

and simultaneously in Canada by Random House of Canada Limited, Toronto. Distributed by Random House, Inc.,

New York. Originally published as a Borzoi Book by Alfred A. Knopf in 1952.

www.randomhouse.com/kids

KNOPF, BORZOI BOOKS, and the colophon are registered trademarks of Random House, Inc.

Library of Congress Cataloging-in-Publication Data

Duvoisin, Roger, 1904–1980

Petunia's Christmas / by Roger Duvoisin.

p.   cm.

SUMMARY: Petunia the goose tries to save a handsome gander from becoming Christmas dinner at Windy Farm.

ISBN 0-394-80868-1 (trade) — ISBN 0-394-90868-6 (lib. bdg.)

[1. Geese–Fiction. 2. Christmas–Fiction.] I. Title.

PZ7.D957Pe 2004

[E]–dc22

2003066100

MANUFACTURED IN MALAYSIA

October 2004   10 9 8 7 6 5 4 3 2 1

The new snow was soft like a kitten's fur. Petunia liked it that way, and she went out for a walk to feel it with her feet. She saw that the deer, the rabbit, the squirrel, were also out in the snow. They were hunting for food.

Petunia went up the hill, through the woods, down the valley,
where she slipped into a tailspin on the frozen stream.

"The country looks all new when it's like this," thought Petunia. "It's lovely like the farmhouse when it's freshly painted." But the walk made her hungry, and she searched for food through the snow.

When she reached Windy Farm, on the other side of the
stream, Petunia was stopped by a call: "Yohoo . . . pssttt . . .
yohoooo . . ."

Who could be calling her? Petunia was very curious. She ran
over to see.

She found a big gander in a small yard enclosed by a wire fence.

"Good day, my name is Charles," said the gander. "You are pretty. Who are you?"

"I am Petunia," said Petunia. "You are handsome."

"I am too fat," sighed Charles. "Being fattened for Christmas. Alas, I fear I'll be roasted and served with apple sauce. Aren't you being fattened too?"

"Pets aren't fattened," said Petunia. "*I* am a pet. Why don't you come with me and be a pet too. Mr. Pumpkin, *my* farmer, is a nice man."

"Oh, I would love it!" cried Charles. "But I am a prisoner. I am too heavy to fly over the fence. And the gate is closed. The farmer's wife opens it when she comes in with my corn, but she always closes it behind her. Ah, Petunia, if you could only help me escape!"

"Of course I will," promised Petunia. "Christmas comes in three weeks. That will give me time to *think* and do something. Wait for me, I'll be back soon."

Petunia plodded back over her tracks. Her heart was full of the handsome gander, and her head full of ideas for freeing him.

Petunia lost no time when she arrived at her farm. She brought the cold-water paint from the toolshop and painted herself into a fairy-tale monster. She looked so fierce that she was afraid to look at herself in the mirror.

Then she returned to Windy Farm, all painted up. The fox came to meet her on the way, for he had smelled goose flesh; but he ran off in fright at the sight of her.

Up at Windy Farm, Petunia waited behind the barn for the
farmer's wife to come out with the corn for Charles. She waited
and waited until her feet were cold; and for goose feet, that's
very, very cold. But the farmer's wife came at last, and as soon
as she had unlocked the gate . . .

Petunia shot out from behind the barn making terrific war-honks.

Honk! Honk! Honk!

"Help! Help! A flying dragon!" shrieked the farmer's wife. She fled to the house. So there . . . the gate was open!

Charles came out. He walked off with Petunia over the hill—free.

But that was not all. The farmer heard his wife's cries and got
his two-barrel gun and went to shoot the flying dragon. He found
the tracks in the snow—Charles' big tracks, and Petunia's. "It's
a goose-footed flying dragon," he muttered. "And it stole my fine
gander." So with his gun cocked, he followed the tracks over the
hill, and through the woods, and right into Mr. Pumpkin's farm.

"Well, neighbor," said Mr. Pumpkin, "what do you want to shoot on my farm with your big gun?"

"The flying dragon that stole my fine gander," said the hunter. "Look! Its tracks lead to your barn . . ."

At that moment, Petunia came out of the barn, honking her loudest honks. But the hunter did not run like his wife, for he had a gun. He aimed it.

"Don't shoot! It's Petunia!" cried Mr. Pumpkin. "I know her voice . . ."

"Petunia? What's that?" asked the hunter, resting his gun.

"She's our pet goose! Why, neighbor, she almost scared me, too!"

While Mr. Pumpkin admired Petunia's war paint, the hunter went into the barn, where he found Charles hidden in a pile of hay.

"You will escape no more," said the hunter as he led Charles away.

"A twenty-pound goose at seventy-five cents a pound, that's more than I can afford to lose."

Poor Petunia,
how she cried!

She loved Charles so.

But then she thought of the
farmer's words: "Twenty pounds
at seventy-five cents."

"Twenty times seventy-five
cents. That's a lot
of money. If I had it,
I could buy Charles's
freedom.

"I am going to earn it."

So Petunia began the easy way—she thought.

But people were too busy to stop and read her sign. They went on about their business, and few pennies dropped into Petunia's cup. She would never earn Charles's freedom that way. Time was too short.

So she went to the woods to gather a load of pine twigs, which she brought to the barn.

The barn smelled nice with the pine scent. Petunia sat among the twigs, and she tied them into beautiful Christmas wreaths with red ribbons.

When she trotted out of town with the wreaths piled all over her, Petunia was the gayest Christmas goose you ever saw.

People liked her so much that they flocked around her like children around a window full of toys.

Everyone wanted Petunia's wreaths. Some even asked whether they could buy her, too. She soon went home with her cup full of coins.

Petunia counted the coins three times on the barn floor, but there were not enough. Not enough to buy all of Charles's twenty pounds. Poor Charles. She must make more wreaths to sell.

Petunia made more wreaths; she made paper angels; she made stars; paper Christmas trees, and other Christmas things. And she went to town again to sell them. At last she had enough money. Even enough to buy a few extra pounds—just in case.

But was it not too late now? Christmas was so near. Petunia
almost flew to Windy Farm with a bag full of coins.

Oh, joy! Charles was still there, in his yard.
The farmer and his wife opened their eyes big as Christmas
tree balls when Petunia offered the bag of coins in exchange for
Charles's freedom.

They were good-hearted. The farmer's wife wiped her eyes
with the corner of her apron when she thought of Petunia's
devotion. They would not take the bag of coins.

"Charles is free," the farmer said. "Keep the coins for a happy
Christmas."

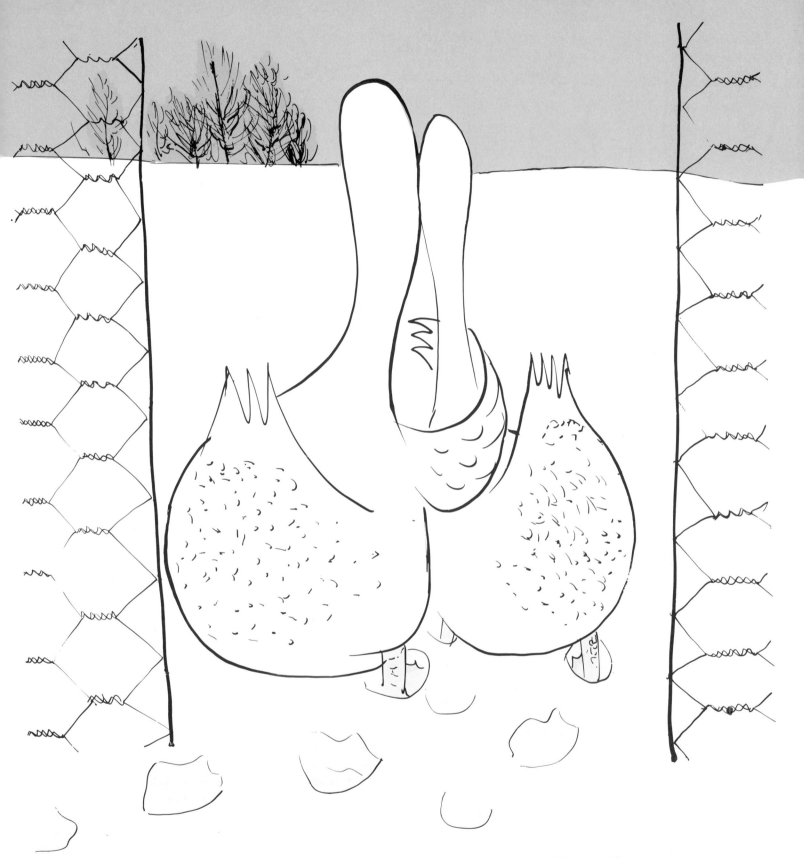

Charles and Petunia thanked the good farmer and his wife,
and they went out together over the hill.

Petunia and Charles were married on Christmas day. The barnyard had never seen so much dancing, singing, and feasting.

It was a very, very merry Christmas.

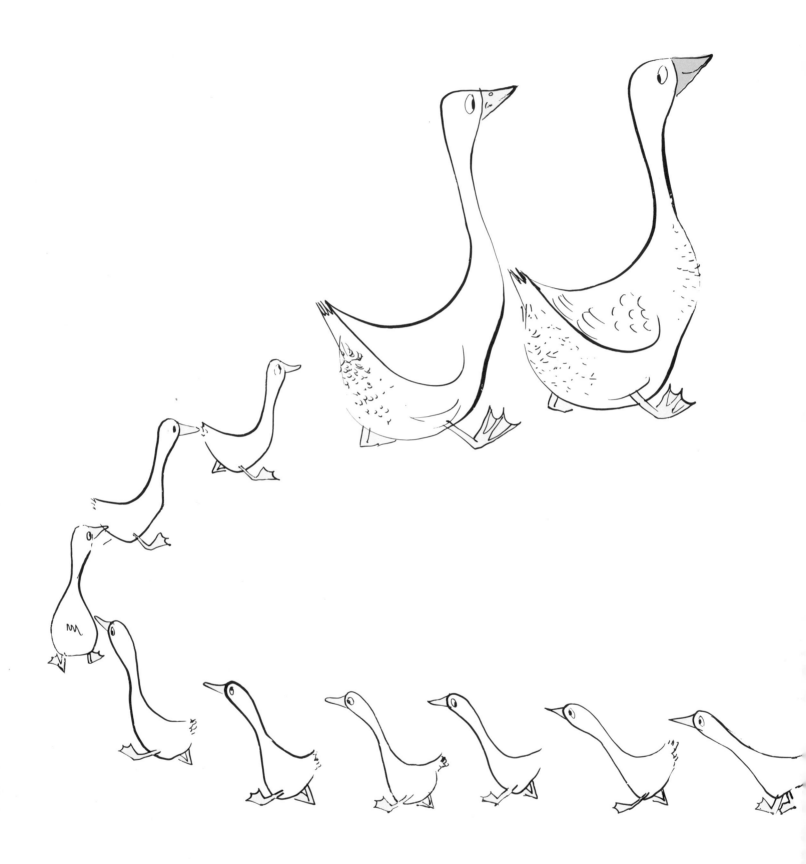

And Petunia and Charles were happy ever after.

ROGER DUVOISIN was born in Geneva, Switzerland, in 1904 and came to the United States in 1925. He wrote and illustrated 40 books—including five books about Petunia—and illustrated more than 100 written by other authors, including *The Happy Lion* by his wife, Louise Fatio. He received the Caldecott Medal in 1948 for *White Snow, Bright Snow* and a Caldecott Honor in 1966 for *Hide and Seek Fog,* both written by Alvin Tresselt. He was also a distinguished magazine illustrator and an important *New Yorker* cover artist starting in 1935. Roger Duvoisin died in 1980.